CW01044163

1

Also by Patrick Langridge.

Bound for carnage

Bound for retribution

THE

FINAL

BOUND

1

We stood there in silence. Neither of us knew what to
say next. I had so many questions, but didn't know
where to start. Then the silence was broken.
"You must have questions. I will gladly answer them,
but first, how are Sally and the girls?"
This was not a question I expected to have to answer.
"I think you should come inside."
I led the way through the gate and up to my place. I was
thankful that the girls were out at that moment. I didn't
want them around for this. They would be out for a few
more hours, so I needed to get my questions answered
and see where we went from there. Once we were inside,
I offered my unexpected guest a drink, then we sat down.
I was still shocked to see who was sitting opposite me.
"Mate. I don't know how to tell you this, So I'll just
come out with it. Sally died a few hours ago. I'm so
sorry."
"What? How? No way. No, this isn't ...."
I took his glass and refilled it. He knocked that back in
one gulp.

"Fill it up" he said, handing me his empty glass.

I went and filled his glass again and refilled mine too. I sat back down and handed him his drink. I'd had to tell Sally her husband was dead. Now I was having to tell John, his wife was dead. This was the weirdest experience of my life. How was he sitting here? Why was he sitting here?

He was just sitting and staring into space. He took a sip of his drink then spoke again.

"What happened?"

"Car crash mate. The person she was in the vehicle with, tried to get her out."

"Did the other person survive?"

"Yes."

"I want to speak with that person."

"You can later. I want to know where the hell you've been for the past couple of years? Why have you not contacted us before now?"

"It's a long story."

"I've got all day." I said.

"I'll tell you. Then I want to speak with whoever was in that vehicle with Sally."

2

JOHN'S STORY

I'd been having threats through my mail. My old security company foiled a robbery a few years ago, and the people who we stopped, wanted revenge for what they lost. Millions of pounds worth of art was what they were after. My security firm stopped them.

To start with, I wasn't that bothered. I thought they were just pissed because we stopped them, and it would soon die down. It soon turned to death threats towards Sally and the girls. Things just kept getting worse, so eventually I decided that faking my death, may make them give up. I didn't know how I was going to do it.

I thought about it for some time. I made sure Sally and the girls would be taken care of. I knew you would give them what I'd asked you to. Knowing they would be alright, made it easier to go through with it. It wasn't meant to be for long. I thought I'd just sort these people out then get back to the girls. That wasn't so easy. Those people weren't easy to track down. I managed to track down some of them, but I knew there was a boss man I needed to find. That was my next part of the plan. That's when that shit happened with you. Will was killed. That bastard Nick knocked me out and tied me up.

I started to think that if he killed me, at least the girls would be ok. By this point I still didn't know how I was going to fake my death. Then we got to the building blowing up. As you know, I wasn't in there long. I noticed a guy sleeping rough in the corner of the area I walked into, then I heard you screaming for me to get out so I ran for it. I didn't even have chance to try and get him out. I only just got out as the explosion happened. It singed my back a little, but I managed to get away. That's when I realised it would be the perfect time to be dead. You would think I'd perished and nobody would be any the wiscr.

I heard another explosion and realised it was a vehicle up the track. I didn't know who was in that vehicle, but I knew it was my chance to get away. I just ran until I was well away from the area. Once I was well away, I sat and got my thoughts together. My back was sore from the blast. My head hurt. I knew I should get medical attention, but that would mean people knowing I was alive. I had to get back to my house and retrieve some kit. I had a secret safe in the floor of my office. Only I knew it was there. After finally making it back to the house, I had to wait until Sally and the girls left. It was hard seeing them getting in the car, going to school. I wanted so much to run over and hug them all but I just couldn't. I planned to deal with the threat quickly then get back to them. Obviously, that took a lot longer than planned. I went into the house and retrieved what I needed. Again, it was hard being in the house, seeing their stuff lying around. I sat on the floor and broke down. This was going to be hard. I couldn't see any other way of dealing with it and keeping Sally and the girls safe. Leaving the house as I found it, I got away from there.

A guy I know sells cars. Not new ones, but decent ones, so I found myself having to steal a car from him. It pained me to be doing that but I had no choice. I just needed to get away. I waited until it was dark, then helped myself. I planned to repay him when I'd sorted things out. Like I said, I dealt with some of those guys but I still needed to find the boss man. Rounding up those guys and dealing with them wasn't something I enjoyed, but it had to be that way. Eventually I found out that the boss man was in America. It was going to be a task to get over here, as I was meant to be dead. I managed to find someone who could get me new ID. I thought about contacting you but that would have put you in a position where you'd have to lie to the girls about my death. I thought it better if I kept you out of it. After a while I was ready to get over here and find this boss man but I went to watch the house one last time to see Sally and the girls, just to find it empty. There was a for sale sign up, so I contacted the estate agent to see if I could find out where they went, but they couldn't tell me. I spent so long looking for them, I almost gave up, thinking they were better off just thinking I was dead. Anyway, eventually I found out they had moved out here. Once I was happy that I would have no problems flying out here, I booked the flight. My plan was to find that gang boss, deal with him, then find Sally and the girls. After finding an address for the guy, I kept an eye on the place for a few days, just to find out he was already dead. Shot in his own back yard apparently. That was the point where I had to decide whether to come back in their lives again, or just let them move on. That's when I contacted you. I was surprised that my message was routed through somebody else, but I'd made contact, so I was happy about that. I thought it best to speak with you first. The meeting at the park was planned. I was there waiting and watching. I saw you at the park, then you disappeared. I remembered you telling me about this place so I decided to see if I could find out where it was. It was only luck that I decided to check around this area first, that I found this place. It looked different than you described but the area seemed right. I knew you wouldn't plan a meet to far away , so I spoke to the guys on the gate and here we are. Its been the worst couple of years of my life. The thought of seeing Sally and the girls again made me happy.

3

He told me pretty much everything he'd been through the last couple of years. I still had questions.

"This place was destroyed thanks to that Nick guy. It was rebuilt, that's why it looks different. I thought you were dead. I nearly got blown up myself. If I hadn't noticed those explosives under my vehicle we wouldn't be talking now. Do you have any idea what it was like trying to explain to Sally what had happened? It was the worst feeling ever. Now I've had to tell you. You should have contacted me. We could have dealt with it together."

"I thought about it, but you had your own shit to deal with. I didn't know what to do, that's why I decided to deal with it myself. Now I wish I had contacted you.

Things may have been different. Sally may still be alive."

John broke down. Cursing at the fact he should have been here with Sally and the girls, not leaving them to deal with the shit while he tried to protect them.

I poured him another drink. He waved it away.

"I don't want to sit here drinking. I want to see the girls."

"Get your head straight mate. Then we can sort that out. You will have a lot of explaining to do to those girls. You need to get it straight what you are going to tell them."

"Do they know about Sally yet?"

"No mate. Haven't had chance to talk to them yet. Not sure how that conversation will go."

"I will tell them." Said John. "I caused this mess. I will deal with it."

"I'm not sure that's a good idea. You walking in there will shock them enough. I should tell them, then we can decide the right time for you to show your face."

"Show my face? Those are my daughters. They have a right to know the truth about what's been going on. If anyone's fucking telling them, it's me."

"I just don't think its fair to throw all this at them at once." I said.

"Look mate, I appreciate what you've done for them but I need to do this. Please just let me do this."

"Ok. Just be gentle with them ok. They lost Sally once briefly. They'd only just got her back. Now this."

"Hold on. What the fuck do you mean, they lost her

once?"

"She was kidnapped. We tracked her down and got her back. She was taken off the street on her way to work with her friend. Her friend didn't make it."

"When did all this happen?"

"This last week. She's only been back a couple of days. She wanted to visit the beauty salon where she and her friend worked. We sent security to watch her, but the kidnappers were watching. She was being driven back here when the car she was in was run off the road. The driver of that vehicle tried to get her out, but he got pushed back by flames."

"So, she burned to death. Fucking hell, that poor woman. If you got her back, how come the kidnappers were still able to find her and do this. I thought that boss man was dead. That should have been the end of it."

"It wasn't that simple mate. That boss man had her kidnapped. The kidnappers weren't aware of his death so they tried to get her back to take her to him. The likelihood is, she died before she burned."

"So, this still isn't over?"

"They probably think it's over but we are gearing up to find them and deal with them."

"You know you aren't doing this without me" said John.

4

I showed John to the girl's room. They had not been home long, this was going to be a horrible end to their day. I wanted to have a word with them first but he insisted in doing this himself, so I left them to it and went to see Billy. I would pop back in a little while and see how they were doing.

We had a few things to plan but first we needed to know where Michael and his guys were.

"Hi mate. How's it going?"

"Getting there." Said Billy.

"Any luck tracking Michael down?"

"He will be hard to find now. But I know of a few places we can check out." Said Dennis, as he walked over.

"Oh hi. Didn't realise you were here."

"Just grabbed a couple of beers from the fridge. You want one?"

"No thanks."

Dennis handed Billy his beer then continued.

"He won't go back to the house in Harrisburg. He knows that will be compromised now. He has a couple of little hide outs that I know of and a cabin in some forest that I've not been to. My guess is that's where he will be. He doesn't necessarily think we will be looking for him. He thinks he's untouchable, so he may not be hiding. I'm not sure where that cabin is but we can check out those other places in the mean time. I will try and find out where it is. I'm pretty sure it's between Payette National Forest and Salmon-Challis National Forest, Idaho."

"If anyone can find it, Billy can. How many men does he have? Once he finds out we are after him, he will use every man he has to take us down. We need to be geared up for a big fight."

"He has a lot of men working for him. If he pulled them altogether, I'd say we are looking at sixty to seventy men."

"Shit. We are going to need a small army to take them. We will need to plan this out thoroughly before we go after him. Give those other two locations to Billy. Billy, can you get us everything you can on those locations, routes in and out. Aeriel photos too, please."

"No problem. I'll have it all ready for you in the morning."

"Your arm any better?"

"Yes. I'll be fine." Said Dennis. "When we get hold of my brother, I want to be the one to deal with him"

"That's fine by me." I said. "I'm going to the armoury to see what we need."

"Can I tag along?" said Dennis.

"Yeah."

"Thanks Billy, I'll catch up with you in the morning." I shouted over my shoulder as we left.

"Am I right in thinking, you plan to take out my brother? Permanently?"

"Don't think we have any choice. It's too much of a risk to let him go. Besides, I don't think he'll go down without a fight."

"Believe me, I don't have a problem with it. Like I said, I'd like to be the one to deal with him."

"Again, I'm happy with that but if you don't go through with it, John will."

"I know."

We arrived at the armoury. It was a big concrete structure, half in the ground. We stepped down in through the main doorway, and through another door into a large area with a corridor down the middle. Little corridors off to the sides. All leading to different rooms full of different weapons, ammunition, body kits, such as Kevlar vests, helmets. Gloves, ammo belts, chest rigs. Rooms for mines. Rooms for explosives. This place was kitted out better than any armoury I went in when I was in the military. Dennis looked absolutely stunned at what was in front of him.

"I can't believe you were worried about needing an army to take Michael down. He has some kit to hand, but not like this. Well not that I know of."

"We need to make sure we are ready for anything. Not sure how many men we will be taking yet but we need to take them by surprise if we can. If not, we go in fast all guns blazing."

We had a chat with the armourer and made a list of the things we needed to put together. Most of the guys working for Stan had their own personal favourite weapon, so the guys we picked to join us, would collect their own personal gear when needed.

After getting all the gear organised, we left the armoury.

"I'm going to see John and the girls. He wants to meet you."

"I'm heading for the canteen. I'll be there for a little while. If I'm not there I'll be in my room if you need me." Said Dennis.

"Ok. We'll find you in a little while." I said.

I knocked and let myself in. The girls were huddled up to John, crying.

"You guys need anything?" I asked.

"We need to catch the son of a bitch who did this."

"We will. I can promise you that."

"You have let him get away before. Don't make promises you can't keep, Mike."

"He won't get away again. We are getting organised to find him and take him out. We can talk about this later. You want me to bring you anything?"

The girls shook their heads, they didn't want anything.

"Some strong coffee would be good right now." Said John.

"I'll head to the canteen and get you some. Be back soon."

I left and made my way to the canteen. When I got there, Dennis and Billy were sat eating. I poured a couple of large mugs of coffee and went over to have a word.

"I don't think John will be up for that chat this evening. Best leave it until tomorrow." I said to Dennis.

"Ok. I'm happy to chat to him whenever."

Billy handed me a mobile phone.

"This is for John. I was going to come and find you once I'd eaten."

"Thanks mate. I Will make sure he gets it."

"I've linked his number to all our phones."

"You are a star as always Billy. I Will let you guys enjoy your supper. I'll pop and see you in the morning Billy."

"No probs. I'll have everything ready for you."

I went back to John and the girls. They had now gone to their own rooms. John was just sat there staring at the floor.

"Here you go mate." I said, handing him his coffee.

"Thanks. The girls are distraught Mike. We can't let that arsehole get away again."

"Trust me, he won't get away again. Once we find him, he's toast. I've told Dennis, the guy who was in the car with Sally, that if he doesn't take out his brother, you will."

"Hold on a minute. The guy she was with, was the kidnappers brother?"

"Sorry mate. Should have mentioned that earlier. Yes, he helped her escape."

"Did he have anything to do with the kidnapping?"

"Not really."

"Stop right there, Mike. Did he or not?"

"I think he should tell you what happened. He was there, I wasn't."

"Right, where is he. I want to talk to him right now."

"Now isn't a good time. I've told him you two can have a chat in the morning."

"Since when did you start keeping things from me Mike?"

"I'm not keeping things from you. It's just better that he tells you what happened."

"First thing Mike. Me and him will chat."

"Yes mate. First thing."

Michael was sat at a table in his hideout.
"I can't fucking believe Reg, is dead.
How did this happen? How did they even get to him?
His place was secure."
"Right now, I couldn't give a fuck. You left my boys on
that hill to die. We have heard nothing from them. They
obviously didn't make it. You have a lot to answer for."
Said Bobby senior.
"Stop fucking whining. They knew what they were
getting into. They fucked up and paid with their lives.
Let it go."
"The hell I will. You think you are untouchable, well
you aren't. You will pay for what you've done."
Bobby dived across the table and grabbed Michael by
the throat. He barely got a grip on him when Michael put
his hands up to Bobby's face and pushed his thumbs into
his eyes. Bobby let out a squeal and let go of Michael's
throat so he could pull his hands away from his eyes.
Michael stood and snatched his hands away and started
to punch Bobby in the face. He was a lot older than
Michael but still put up a good fight. He didn't fight for
long, before Michael knocked him out.
"Get this piece of shit tied up and lock him in one of the
rooms. I'll deal with him later." He told two of his guys.
They ran over and took Bobby away.
Michael was trying to think of how he was going to get
his brother. He wasn't about to let him get away with
what he'd done. Ever since they were kids, Michael had

always looked after Dennis. Their parents were hardly ever around. When they were around, they were always getting drunk or high on the shit they used to smoke. Michael would always be the one to get a hiding if himself or Dennis got out of line. He knew he had to take care of his little brother and he just took the beatings, so Dennis didn't have to. Eventually their mother overdosed and their father was never around. He woke up one morning, grabbed a few things and left with Dennis. Dennis always looked up to Michael until he started working for Reg. From that point on, Michael changed. He got violent easily. He started drinking a lot. They did a lot of dirty jobs for Reg, but once Michael had beaten that poor woman to death, Dennis knew he would have to lead his own life. He didn't want any part of that life anymore. After helping Sally escape, he decided that he would get his life in order, and hoped that one day he would settle down and get married, possibly have kids too.

Michael had other ideas. He wasn't going to let it go. He would take out his brother and his new friends. He didn't realise just how difficult that was going to be.

I'd asked Dennis to come over to my place once he's had breakfast. This conversation between him and John was not going to be a pleasant one. I decided it would be best if they had their chat in private away from all the other guys. After inviting Dennis over, I decided it would be best if I hung around. John would not like what Dennis had to tell him, I needed to be there to stop things kicking off. I could understand how John would see it but at the same time, Sally may have been dead sooner if Dennis hadn't helped her escape. We had to give him credit for that at least.

He knocked on the door and I went to let him in.

"Hi mate, Come in."

"Is John here?"

"He is through here." I said as I led him through the door to my living room.

"John meet Dennis."

Dennis walked over to where John was sitting and outstretched his hand.

John just sat there without saying anything.

"Take a seat mate" I said to Dennis, pointing to one of the armchairs.

"I will be in the kitchen if you need anything."

Leaving the room, I shut the door and left them to it.

"What do you want to know?" said Dennis.

"I want to know why my wife died while she was with you."

"I was trying to save her. We were being chased and I was trying to get her back here. We got rammed off the road. I tried to get her out but the flames were just too much."

John watched as Dennis rubbed his face, and the burns on his arm. They were going to leave nasty scars. He was thankful that Dennis was there to try and free her but what was she doing there with him in the first place. "Why was she even with you? Why was she being chased?"

Dennis took a deep breath to relax himself. He knew that John was not going to like what he was about to tell him. "She was kidnapped by my brother. I was there. I was at the house where we kept her and her friend. They weren't going to be there long. She was going to be handed over to my brother's boss. And used to get money from you."

"You held her for some kind if ransom?"

"Not really. They were going to use her to get to you. She told my brother that you were no longer alive so they decided they would get what they were owed, from her instead."

"My security company stopped a multi million pound robbery. We owe your brother, or whoever he was working for, nothing!"

"I know that. The boss man didn't care. He wanted pay back for what you did. The girl who was picked up with Sally was beaten to death by my brother. I knew from that point that I had to get her out of there before he tried to do it to her. We managed to get away only to be tracked and found by Mike and his friends. They found us just hours before my brother did. They helped us get away after being shot at. We were followed for a while until they were taken care of. I was shot but Sally helped me by stopping the bleeding and looking after me on the flight back here."

"You all got back here safely. Why was it that she ended up in a car with you, being chased then?"

"After a couple of days Sally wanted to go to the salon that she worked at, to see the girls there. The girl my brother killed also worked there so she just wanted to tell them what had happened and help them arrange a memorial for her. We had a couple of security guys with us. They waited outside in their car. It wasn't long before one of them rushed in and told us to get back in the car quickly. When we got back outside one of the security guys was shot by some guys in an SUV. The other security guy tossed me his car keys and told me to get her back here. One of the SUV's followed us and then another joined the chase. We were so close to making it, before they started trying to push us off the road. Eventually I lost control and we went over the edge and rolled down the side of the hill. Once the car settled, I managed to get out and ran round to try and get her out. I kept trying even when the flames started but eventually it got too hot. I'm sorry I couldn't get her out. I don't know what happened after that, I must have passed out because the next thing I remember was waking up in the medical bay here."

John sat there without saying a word. It was a couple of minutes before he stood up and jumped towards Dennis.

He grabbed him by the collar and threw his fist back ready to punch him.

"If you hadn't kidnapped her in the first place, she would still be alive." John shouted as tears welled up in his eyes.

"They were after you. This all happened because of you. If we hadn't taken her someone else would have and she may have died sooner."

Dennis sat there waiting for the punch to come. He could see John's knuckles whitening as he was tensing his fist.

After hearing shouting, I opened the door and saw John holding Dennis with his fist raised. They needed to sort this out themselves or they wouldn't be able to work together. I would jump in if I had too.

They stared at each other for what seemed like a lifetime. Eventually John let go, stood up and walked out. He rushed past me and out through the main door.

Dennis stood and went to follow.

"Leave him mate. He just needs to cool off."

"We can't leave it like this."

"If he wanted to take it further, he would have. Something stopped him so lets give him some space. He'll come around when he's ready."

8

I took Dennis to see Billy. If he was with me, he couldn't go after John. We needed to get going with the hunt for his brother, and Billy was always the one we could rely on for information.

"Morning Billy. How's it going?"

"If you mean, how are things in general? not bad. If you mean, as far as the search is going? Not so good. We've just had confirmation that Michael is not back at the old house, or that other location Dennis gave us. We need to find that cabin you were talking about." He said looking at Dennis.

"Not sure I can help there. I've never been there, just heard about it."

"That place could be anywhere. How are we going to even start to know where to look?" I said to both of them.

"Beats me. I'll keep the drones in the air but it's not looking good. We need more information." Said Billy.

"There may be a way, but I'm not sure it'll work." Said Dennis.

"If you have any ideas right now, we are all ears." I said.

"There are a couple of guys who are working for Michael, that may be able to help. I know their numbers."

"Not sure that is a good idea. If they get any trace where you are calling from, we wont have to worry about finding them."

"This may work." Said Billy. "We can call them on a secure phone with no traceability. Or we can get Dennis to call using a traceable phone at a location that suits us."

"You mean draw them to us?"

"Exactly that."

"Billy, you are a genius."

"That's what I do." Billy said with a grin on his face.

"Where would we need to be, to do it that way?" asked Dennis.

"That's what we need to figure out." I said.

"How about we try the untraceable phone idea first. See what we get. If that doesn't work. We draw them in."

"Ok lets do that. Sort out the phone and let us know when its ready."

"No need. I prepared a couple earlier."

"You really do think of everything."

"Like I said..."

"Yes, we know. That's what you do." I said smiling.

We all had a little chuckle. It was nice to see people laughing for a change. There wasn't much of that happening lately.

"Ah, nearly forgot. Stan wants to be involved. He said not to go anywhere without him."

"Thought he was all loved up now. Why would he want to jump back into the action?"

"You know Stan. That's what he's always done. He said it's more personal this time. What with Sally and John's involvement."

"Ok we'll keep him in the loop once we know what the plan is."

"Are you ready to make that call?" Billy asked. Handing over a mobile phone to Dennis.

"No time like the present."

Dennis put in a number and waited for an answer. None came. He put in a different number and waited. This time it was answered.

9

Bobby was sitting on a chair in the room he'd been locked in. His hands were tied before he was thrown in the room but he made light work of getting out of his bonds. He decided not to try and break out of the room at this time. He would use the time to come up with a plan. Some of the guys were still loyal to him, he was sure of it. He just had to let them know what his plan was. He was sure they would help.

The phone in his pocket started to ring. He pulled out the phone and looked at the screen. No caller ID.

"Who the fuck? Hello."

"Hi Bobby. I was hoping you'd answer."

Bobby knew that voice but could not place it.

"Who are you?"

"It's Dennis."

"You've got to be fucking shitting me. Do you have any idea what kind of shit storm you've caused? If I was you, I'd run away. Far away."

"Listen to me Bobby. I need your help."

"You need my help? My boys are dead because of this shit. Your lucky I don't find you and put a bullet in you myself."

"Fuck. I'm sorry Bobby. I didn't know they were dead."

"Like you'd fucking care anyway."

"I had no choice but to do what I did. Michael is out of control. I'm done with that shit."

"What do you want Dennis?"

"I need to know where Michael is."

"What, are you going to come and tell him what a bad person he is?" Bobby laughed at his own sarcasm.

"Seriously Bobby. Where is he?"

"I'm not sure telling you is a good idea. You will get yourself killed if you pick a fight with your brother. You know that."

"I'm not picking a fight. I have some friends here who want to find him. They will find him either way. I was just hoping you would help me. You don't like him anyway. He's always giving you shit."

"Just who are these so-called friends of yours?"

"The ones who helped me and the girl get away."

"Those same arseholes are the ones who killed my boys."

"Look, I'm sorry about them. I really am, but Michael needs to be stopped and you know it."

Bobby just sat there for a few seconds without saying anything.

"What makes you think your friends can take Michael down?"

"You'll just have to trust me Bobby, Please. Help us find him"

"Look. I'm having some issues with that brother of yours myself right now. I don't know if you being back in the picture will make things worse. Give me a number that I can contact you on and I'll think about it and call you back."

"You know I cant do that. Just tell me you will help."

"You call me for help, now you suddenly don't trust me to have your number."

"Its not you I don't trust."

"Call me back in a few hours."

"Thanks Bobby, I appreciate it."

"I've agreed to nothing yet."

Bobby ended the call. He now had two options. He could help Dennis or he could play Michael and Dennis against one another. He felt good, this will help him get out of this situation and deal with Michael at the same time. As for Dennis, he wasn't sure what he was going to do.

10

"Did you get it?" Dennis asked.

"No. Looks like his phone is untraceable too."

"Damn it." I said. "that's all we can do right now. We'll see what he has to say later. We have Sally's memorial tomorrow, let's make sure everything is ready for that. I need to go and catch up with Danny. I'll See you guys in a bit"

I left Billy's place and walked over to the main building. After not seeing Danny for a couple of days, I wanted to catch up and keep him in the loop about Dennis's brother. I found him in the canteen stuffing his face as usual. Pouring myself a coffee I looked over to see if he wanted another. He shook his head so I went to join him.

"How's thing going?" he said.

"Still struggling to get a location for Michael. Dennis contacted one of Michael's guys, so we're hoping he can help locate him."

"You think he will help?"

"Dennis seems to think he will. They will be talking again later, so we'll see what happens."

"How's John doing?"

"As expected I guess. He's not in a good place right now. We need to find Michael and take him out, hopefully that will help John get to grips with the situation."

"can't imagine how he's feeling right now."

"We'll just have to keep an eye on him. Is Sally's memorial all sorted?"

"Yes mate. It's all organised. All we need to do is turn up. One thing though, John's memorial is still there."

"Shit, I forgot about that. Maybe we should try and get that Taken down before the memorial tomorrow."

"Well, I've been thinking about that. Maybe we should just leave it for now. Michael thinks he is dead so maybe we should just leave it there a while longer. Just for show."

"I see what you mean. May work in our favour. Whether it helps or not, a little while longer won't hurt."

"Yes, I agree."

"We had those other two locations checked out for Michael. Looks like he has a new hiding spot. Let's hope Billy and Dennis can find it."

"If anyone can, Billy can. You still trust Dennis?"

"He hasn't given me any reason not to so far. He nearly died helping Sally, so I think we can trust him."

"Lets hope you're right. So what's next?"

"We wait and see how Dennis's call goes later. We have the memorial in the morning, so we won't get anything else done today I shouldn't think."

"Let me know how it goes."

"I'll let you know when it's happening, we can both go to Billy's and listen in."

"Sounds good."

I left the canteen and went to look for John. He'd had a bit of time to cool down now, hopefully he was in the mood to chat.

After checking the twins place and having a quick chat with them, I went to my place and that's where I found him.

"How are you doing?"

"Its just a lot to take in. It's emotional seeing the girls after all this time, plus Sally's death. Just can't get my head around it."

"Yeah, it's all happening at once. You want a drink?"

"Why not."

I poured us some drinks and went and sat in the other chair.

"This memorial tomorrow, we realised that your memorial is still there. We think it's best to keep it there a little longer, just until this shit is dealt with."

"Whatever. Makes no difference to me."

"Just thought I'd let you know. May feel weird seeing it tomorrow."

John nodded and took a slurp of his drink. His memorial was the least of his worries right now.

"You any closer to finding that piece of shit?"

"Not yet. We are still working on it. Dennis is in contact with someone who works with his brother."

"Work?" John laughed hard at that. "They don't work, they just make people's lives a misery."

"I agree. Once Dennis talks to this guy later, we may know more."

"You think he will just tell Dennis where they are and it'll all be over with?"

"Not at all, but this is all we have to work with right now."

11

Underneath Michael's hideout was a cave system left behind from an old mine. It consisted of three tunnels all joining up at a central cave. All the old machinery had been stripped out years ago so it was stripped bare, that was until Michael found out about it and decided to make use of it. Now the central cave was where all the weapons and vehicles were kept. Originally there were three entrance/exits to this cave. Now only two remained. Michael used one to get from his basement to one of the tunnels, from there he would use a small buggy to get him to the main central cave. The only other way in or out was from the end of tunnel two, that takes you back out on to a hidden track back down the mountain side. This one couldn't be seen from the outside as it was hidden behind false rockery and trees. He was now in the central cave, making sure they were ready if they needed to be. Michael wasn't one for underestimating people. He was confident in his abilities but always prepared for the worst. Dennis got the better of him once before, he wasn't going to let that happen again.

"Boss. Bobby want's to talk with you." Said one of Michael's guys.

"Tell Bobby to fuck off. I have more important things to deal with right now."

"He said to tell you that he is in contact with Dennis." Michael stopped what he was doing. His jaw clenched, as he turned round to look at his guy.

"How the fuck is he in contact with Dennis?"

"No idea boss. He just told me to tell you."

Michael waved the guy away. If Bobby was trying to wind him up, he'd picked the wrong day. He walked back to his buggy and went back up to his cabin.

Bobby had managed to convince the two guys guarding his room, to help him. He would need more men soon but for now he had help. When Michael got back to his cabin, he had the guys bring Bobby to him.

"You trying to wind me up? How can you possibly be in contact with Dennis?"

"He called me. He is meant to be calling me back any time now."

"Why would he call you?"

"He wants to know where you are."

"So you are helping him now are you? And you told me this why?"

"Look, we've had our fall outs but that little shit brother of yours has caused a shit storm. If he thinks I'm helping him, we can get our hands on him."

"So now you are helping me too?"

"Lets just put this shit behind us and get hold of your brother and his new friends, and end this. I'm getting to old for this bullshit."

"You expect me to believe you?"

"Look Michael, he will be calling soon. You can listen in but he mustn't know, or he won't trust me."

"Ok, I'll sit here and listen. Then we will decide what to do about it."

12

Danny and I went down to Billy's. I decided against taking John with me, he wouldn't help the situation right now. Dennis was already there.

"Hi guys" said Billy. "we're ready when you are."

"Lets get it done." I said.

Billy checked that the phone was connected to the computer, then put it on loud speaker.

When he was ready, he gave Dennis a nod.

"Bobby?"

"Who else would it be?"

"I wasn't sure you would answer."

"Well I did. Tell me what your plan is."

"So you are going to help me?"

"I never said that. First, I want to know what you plan to do."

"I've already told you. We want to take Michael down and end all this shit."

"Yes but how do you plan to do it. You think you can just waltz in here and kill him?"

"Not just me, but yeah."

Bobby could see that Michael was raging and he had to put finger to his lips to remind Michael to keep quiet.

"You are being foolish Dennis. You know you won't make it out of here alive."

"Just let me worry about that. You going to help us or not?"

Michael nodded at Bobby to tell him to go along with it.

"Yes, I'll help you. I don't know what you expect me to do. Your brother has me locked up in a room. We had a fall out. I don't know what use I'll be?"

"He can't lock you up like that. What's his problem?"

"That doesn't matter right now. I need to be able to contact you."

"I will text you a contact number. Tell me where you are, I can help."

"I need to find that out myself. Text me your number, as soon as I have the location I'll let you know."

"Ok, I'll send it now. Don't take to long Bobby. I want this dealt with."

"I'll be in touch."

The call ended and Billy was busy tapping keys.

"Still no trace."

"We'll just have to wait for the location." I said.

"You can message him the number now." Billy told Dennis. "It's untraceable so he won't know where you are."

"Ok, doing it now."

"I guess we wait. Hopefully we will have a location soon. Remember, he could be playing us so we have got to be prepared."

"I don't think Bobby would do that to me but I agree, doesn't hurt to be cautious."

"Right, I'm going to get some shut eye. We have to be up early for this memorial in the morning. As soon as I get back from there I'll come and see you."

"Ok, we'll be here."

I left them to it and headed back to mine. It was going to be a shit morning and probably a long day so I planned to get some sleep.

13

After Bobby ended the call, Michael was straight on him.

"Why did you feel the need to tell him I had you locked up?"

"If he thinks me and you aren't on the same page he won't suspect me as a threat. That may be helpful."

"So you think I'm just going to forget you tried to strangle me and let you roam free again?"

"Right now, I'm the only connection you have to Dennis."

"What if I just lock you back up, take your phone, and deal with this myself?"

"You think he will just come here and see you face to face? If he thinks I'm helping him, he will be more likely to make a mistake. We can plan a trap and get him, and his new friends."

Michael thought about this. Bobby was making sense with what he was saying.

"Ok, these two will watch your every move. If you think of betraying me you, will be shot no questions."

"Fair enough. I want Dennis as much as you do. My boys would still be alive if he hadn't taken that girl."

"At least we agree on something. Give Dennis the location and let me know what he plans to do. We will be ready for him."

Michael got up out of his chair and walked to the door. Before he walked through he turned round.

"Do not betray me." He said to Bobby with cold eyes. Then he left.

Bobby stood there with the two guards.

"That was easier than I thought it would be. I appreciate you two staying loyal to me but we will need more men. Can you get more?"

"Yes boss." One of the guards said. "There are a lot of guys here that are loyal to you. We will talk to them and have them be ready to act when needed."

"Excellent. Make sure they don't give anything away, tell them to keep doing what they're doing until we say otherwise."

"Will do boss."

"Appreciate it boys. Don't get caught. Remember, you are meant to be watching me."

Both men nodded.

Bobby messaged Dennis with their current location and hoped that this would work out how he wanted it too.

"What we need, is a layout of this place. Is there any blue prints or anything like that around that you know of?"

"Not that we know of. If there are any papers lying around they are likely to be in the old office in the main central cave."

"Shit. That's not going to be easy to get into."

"Boss, may I suggest that we tell Michael that we need plans to set a trap for his brother?"

"That may work. We can try that, if that fails we will have to scout the place out ourselves and make a plan. Remember, we want to be hidden out of the way when the shit hits the fan."

"I know this place reasonably well boss. Been here a few times now. Had to guard the perimeter a few times."

"Ok good. I think that will help. We can forget asking Michael for plans. Just figure this out ourselves. Tonight when I'm sleeping, one of you needs to go and talk to the loyal ones. Once we know how much help we have, we can make a plan. We can't just lead Dennis here and hide. We need to get the fight started then keep out of the way."

"Ok boss. I'd say we will have fifteen to twenty men willing to help."

"That's not exactly an army but we will make do."

"Can you draw me a layout as best you can? Then we can start looking at things."

"I will have that for you later."

"Good man."

"Lets go and get something to eat."

The two guards followed Bobby to get some food. They had a lot of work ahead of them.

14

We arrived back from the memorial. It was a lovely service. John was a little freaked out by seeing his own memorial but other than that it went well.
John and the girls went back to their room and I went back to mine to change. I'm not a massive fan of wearing a shirt and tie, so as soon as I can, I change.
After changing I went to get coffee.
Dennis and Billy were in the canteen stuffing their faces.

"Hello gents. How's it going?" I said as I sat at their table.

"Hi Mike. We have a location for Michael." Said Dennis.

"Excellent. Have you looked yet?"

"Not yet. That's the next job once we're done here." said Billy.

"I'll come with you when you go. I want to see where that bastard is hiding out. Can we trust this guy?"

"I think we can. My brother has him locked up after they had a fall out. I'm pretty sure he'd like to see the end of him too."

"Ok. Well, like I said last night. We need to be prepared in case he plans to fuck us over just to get to you."

"Stan wants in, like I said before. Once we know where the location is, he wants to be involved."

"I'll go and talk to him once we know where we are going."

"Let's go and look now." Said Billy.

We all stood up and Billy lead the way down to his place. Once there, Dennis read out the coordinates to Billy from the message. He put them through the computer and we waited for it to show us the location.

"Here we go. Now coming up. It's between Payette National Forest and Salmon-Challis National Forest, Idaho."

"Isn't that a mountainous region?"

"Kind of. Some big hills in that area. The terrain is up and down. We are looking at just over a thousand miles away."

"Going to be a slog this one. God knows how many hours driving and a lot of walking when we get there by the looks of it."

"Sounds like we need a quicker way in" said Stan, as he walked over to where they were standing. "What are we looking at here?"

Billy turned the screen so Stan could take a look.

"I see what you mean. Well, we can send some in by helicopter. Get a recce done while they wait for the rest to get there."

"That's actually a good idea. We can guide them in and surround the place." I said.

"Can you narrow it down Billy?" asked Stan.

"The computer is scanning the area. Once it finds something that looks like it could be lived in, it'll let me know. May take a while."

"If it doesn't, what then?" asked Dennis.

"Then I guess we have a bigger area to search on foot."

"That could take days searching that forest area. Can we get the drones up there?"

"We can but we need to get them in the area before we launch them. They don't have enough power to get all that way and then do a search."

"We are going to have to send the drones with whoever goes in the helicopter. They will have to use them as part of their recce." Said Stan.

"Agreed. I will be going in first with a small team. Dennis should come with me."

"You can take Danny and John with you too, and two others. I will lead the rest in when we get to the area. We will all have personal Comms so we can keep in contact all the time."

"Sounds like a plan." I said.

"I don't think we should tell Bobby, the guy I'm in contact with, the exact plan. Give him a rough idea but not too much information."

"Agreed. We need to see if he is with us or against us first."

"Once we are organised, we'll give him an idea of what we plan to do. Hopefully we can meet up with him before we go in." Said Stan.

"I don't think we should rely on him helping anyway. Make a plan that doesn't need him. If he ends up helping, all the better." I said.

"Agreed" was the answer from them all.

"I'm going to talk to John, tell him what's going on and get him to the armoury to kit him out. Let me know when, or if we get a better location."

I left them to it and walked back to see John.

Hopefully we'll get an exact location soon and then it will be all hands on deck. Once we were all organised with our kit, we would be ready to go.

15

Michael was looking at what he would need to do, to defend the place. He couldn't believe that Dennis would soon be walking right into his grasp. He thought he was going to have to hunt him down. This was going to be easier than he thought. He would have to keep an eye on Bobby. He didn't trust him anymore. He would need him for now, at least until Dennis turned up. Then, he would dispose of them both.

"Check the back entrance. Make sure it's still hidden. I don't want it breached when the shit hits the fan but I want it to be ready to drive out of if we need to." He said to one of his guys.

"Yes boss. On it."

Bobby and his two guards walked into the main cave area.

"This is bigger than I remember."

Michael hadn't seen them arrive and swivelled round to face them.

"What are you doing down here?"

"We've come to help set things up."

"I don't need your help. Go back up to the cabin."

"Just want to do my bit."

"Well you are not needed. If I need you, I'll call for you."

Bobby shook his head. Michael was an arrogant prick but Bobby had to play along for now.

"On second thoughts, you, take this up to the old office and give it to the guys in there." Michael said to one of Bobby's guards.

"Yes boss." Came the reply.

Michael handed him a small metal case and the guard scurried away to the old office.

"There must be something I can help with?" asked Bobby.

"Just go up to the cabin, out of my way."

Bobby and his one remaining guard turned and walked back the way they'd come. Bobby was hoping to get near the office to look for blue prints for the mine. There had to be some. Now, one of his men had the opportunity. Just had to hope he could pull it off. Bobby's other Guard walked through the old office door to see only one man in there. That would make things a little easier.

"Michael asked me to bring you this. You need any help?"

"Actually yes, you can lay these wires out across the floor. I need to go and get another reel because we haven't quite got enough here."

"Ok. What are they for?"

"That case you just brought to me contains enough explosives to bring this office and half the cave down with it."

"Why are you rigging explosives in here?"

"The boss wants everything ready to be destroyed if needed. I'll be back in a minute." With that, the man left the office.

Now was his chance. He rummaged through old desk drawers and old filing cabinets looking for the plans. There was nothing there but old papers and rubbish. "They must be here somewhere." He thought to himself. "What are you looking for?" said a voice behind him. The man had returned with the extra wire.

"I was just looking for some plans for this place. Michael needs them."

"Oh. He never mentioned them to me. Probably be in one of those rubbish bags over there. We cleared some

bits out earlier to make room for this lot." He said,
nodding towards the wire and the explosives.

"I'll have a look."

"First, lay these wires out."

He laid the wires out across the floor like he'd been
asked.

"That ok?"

"Yes, perfect."

He walked over to the rubbish bags and rummaged
through them until he finally found what he was looking
for. He put them into his waste band out of sight and
walked out of the office. He hoped that guy didn't
mention the plans to Michael.

He made his way back up to the cabin.

Once he was there, Bobby asked him how he got on.

The guard pulled out the plans with a grin on his face

"Nice. I knew you wouldn't let me down." Said Bobby.

"Let's take them back to the room and have a look. Then
we just need to know how many men we have on our
side.

"I'll go and speak to some of them now."

"Ok. Remember to keep a low profile. We can't have
anyone suspecting you of anything.

"I'll be careful boss."

16

I explained the situation to John and we went through a few scenarios. All he cared about was getting hold of Dennis's brother and making him pay for Sally's death. John was beating himself up over the fact he wasn't around when it all happened. Getting hold of Michael was going to be the only thing to make him feel better about himself.

Billy messaged me and told me he wanted to see us as soon as we were done.

We went straight down to see him.

"Ah good, you're here." Said Billy as we walked in.

"I may have a location for Michael's hideout."

Danny and Dennis walked in to join us.

"Ok Billy. Show us what you have."

Billy put his computer feed onto the new big screen he had on one of his walls.

"Ok gents, this area here has a little cabin and a perimeter fence that looks like it belongs around the perimeter of a military base. I had a friend of mine do me a favour and fly a small military reconnaissance drone over the location we were given. Now, apart from the cabin and fencing it doesn't look like there is much there." Billy tapped a few keys on his keyboard and the camera feed we were looking at, turned into infrared.

"These are the same images, only this time we can just make out some sort of tunnel system underneath the cabin. I've done some research and it turns out, there was once a small mine inside that hillside. The mine has long since closed but some of the tunnels remain. You can see by the feed that there is a very slight heat source in the tunnels and inside what I can only assume is some kind of central area. The drone never picked up any movement or vehicles but it's safe to assume there is definitely something going on in there. This cabin is the only thing visible in that location from the drone."

"You think Michael is hiding underneath that cabin?"

"I'd bet my life on it." Said Dennis. "I knew he had a cabin somewhere in that kind of terrain. That has to be where he is."

"That heat source wouldn't be there unless it was being used for something. That mine has laid dormant for years, it would show no heat source if it was left alone."

"Looks like we have our location. We just need a plan of attack." I said.

"We need to take it from all sides. Sneak up there, then hit them hard." Said John.

"I agree," said Dennis. "We should assume Michael will be expecting us. Don't underestimate him. If he gets cornered, he will fight his way out or die trying."

"That's one thing we can be sure of." Said John.

Dennis looked at him with an irritated look on his face.

"What? I'm just saying what we are all thinking."

"Us four and two others will be going in by chopper. We will be dropped at the foot of the neighbouring hillside and we will go in on foot. Once we have established the outside area is safe, Stan will be leading more guys up from the other side. They will leave here a few hours before us, and once they get there we should already be in position to watch them in."

"That's only two sides covered." Said Danny.

"Stan's team will split in two. We will have the rear and both sides covered then we can hopefully go in through the front door. He won't expect that."

"Let's hope you're right. If you go in under cover of darkness you will be harder to see until you are right on top of them. Use night vis and take your time, you'll be on top of them before they know what's hit them." Said Billy.

"Won't they hear the chopper?" asked Dennis.

"If we keep low behind the neighbouring hillside, they won't hear us, not even at night. Adrian is one of the best pilots I know. He will get us in there." Said Danny.

"Right then, we need to make sure we are all geared up. If everyone agrees, we should leave as soon as we are geared up. It could take Stan and the guys in the vehicles, 17 hours ish to get there. If we follow on a little later and plan to get there by dark tomorrow evening, we can be in position when Stan and the others get there on foot. We'll need to refuel on route anyway."

Everyone agreed and went of to get ready.

17

After seeing Stan and the guys off, the rest of us double checked our gear and milled about for a while. We needed to make sure we were at the drop off and in position before Stan and the rest of them got there. We didn't want to get there too soon as there was more chance of being noticed. We needed to get in, guide the others in and crack on.

I walked over to where Dennis was checking his gear.

"You any good with that?" I asked. Nodding towards the crossbow he'd opted for from the armoury.

"Yes. Better than anyone I know. I thought this would come in handy when we get dropped off. Silent killer."

"Good thinking. The longer we can keep it from going noisy, the better."

"My thoughts exactly."

"How much ammo do you have for it?"

Dennis lifted a belt from the floor.

"This belt holds fifteen bolts. We will probably be making a noise before I use them all anyway."

"There is a good chance of that, yes."

"When you're ready, head over to the heli hanger. I want to have a quick chat with you all before we head out."

"Will do."

I left Dennis to finish getting organised and went to check on everyone else.

An hour later we all convened in the hanger.

"Ok gents, we all know what we need to do. Just keep your eyes open and watch each others backs. Remember, this is a shoot to kill mission. If they aren't with us, Take em out. Any questions?"

Everyone shook their heads. "Ok, saddle up"

We all went outside and climbed aboard the helicopter. I gave Adrian the pilot the thumbs up, and he prepared for lift off. Once we were in the air, we would try and get a bit of shut eye. You never know when the next time for a sleep will come.

Stan and the others had been on the road for a few hours now. They didn't plan on stopping unless absolutely necessary and would pick up food only when stopping for fuel. The plan was for them to keep going so they could get to where they needed to be, just as it got dark. They would then hike in to where we needed them. Once we were all in position, we would start the assault.

18

Bobby and one of his guards were in his room looking over the blue prints for the underground tunnel system, when his other guard came back.

"Boss, we have guys ready to help. Only 15 but I know we can trust them."

"Ok good. We think we've found another exit but it'll be blocked from when the old mine closed down. We can't go out through the cabin door because of all the patrols out there. We can't go out through the main back entrance because Michael has that covered too, so we'll have to try and get out through the blocked exit. It looks like it was filled with rocks and left closed off."

"Could we dig ourselves out?"

"That depends on how big the rocks are. We need to get a couple of guys over there to have a look. If we can't dig our way out, we'll have to blow our way out. Then all hell will break loose."

"I'll have a couple of them go take a look. It may be easier to go out through the cabin and fight our way through.

"Send the guys to check out that exit route then organise weapons and ammo. If we have to go out through the front door, we do it after dark."

"On it."

The guard hurried off to get organized.

"What's the plan then, boss?" asked his other guard.
"Once we know our exit route, we go after dark. We need to be ready to fight, whatever route we take."

19

Michael was doing his usual rounds, making sure everything was ready. He knew they would turn up at some point and he wanted to be prepared.
"Boss. We have a helicopter sighting on one of the perimeter camera's."
"What the hell is a helicopter doing near here? Can you tell what it is?"
"Its a good size boss. Hard to see any detail in the dark but it's behind the east side ridge."
"Get some men over there. Tell them to watch and keep us informed what's going on."
"Yes boss."
Michael was both excited and nervous now. He didn't know what the helicopter was doing here but he had a suspicion that it was something to do with his brother. He'd been waiting for this. Dennis and his friends were going to pay for what they'd done. If Dennis thought he could come here and talk his way out of this, he was sadly mistaken.
"Boss. The men will be there in a couple of minutes."
"Bring up every camera feed that covers that area. I want to see what's going on."
"Only two boss but we should be able to see what's happening."

The camera feeds came up side by side on the screen both men were looking at.

"This one will be where our guys should be in a minute. This one picked up the helicopter." The man pointed to the left and right camera feeds on the screen.

"Here's our guys coming into view now. Looks like the helicopter is behind the ridge, because we can't see it."

"Connect us on speaker, I want to hear what's going on."

"Boss. The helicopter is just hovering behind the ridge. It's like it's waiting for something."

"Do you see anyone.?"

"Not yet boss. We have night vision on but it's just hovering there. Oh wait, looks like it's about to touch down. Yes boss. It's touched down. There are people jumping out. I count six. There may be more but that's all I can see from here."

"Are they armed?"

"It looks like they are armed boss. Yes, I can see now. They are definitely armed. I repeat, they are definitely armed."

"Shit. Ok, listen up. You are to treat them as hostiles. You do not let them get in here. Is that clear?"

"Yes boss. We will take them out."

"And take out that helicopter."

Michael and his guy were watching the screens. They could see their men running around taking up defensive positions. Then, on the right hand screen, they could make out the air wash from the rotor blades of the helicopter as it rose up above the ridge line.

"Do not let that helicopter leave." Michael shouted.

They could see the helicopter turning to go, when it exploded and a bright light lit up the camera feeds.

"Helicopter down"

"Good. Take out those on foot."

"Do you think there will be more?" asked his man.

"We should assume there are more and be ready. Get everyone into their positions. No one gets in here."

20

We eventually got to our drop off point. We would have to wait until Stan and the others were close before beginning our assault.

We soon got a message saying they were on foot and on their way.

"Adrian take us down. We will wait on the ground. Once we are out, take this bird out of the way. We will radio you when we need you"

"Will do."

Adrian gently set the helicopter down and we all jumped out. Once we were on the ground, I signalled for Adrian to go. As he rose up and turned to leave, what looked like an RPG, shot from the ridge and took out the helicopter. We all ducked and turned away from the blast.

"Fuck. Ok, defensive positions. We are clearly going to have to fight our way in but we need to wait for Stan and the others. We keep down and out of sight. If we have to get into a fight, we try and hold them here until the others are in the area to help us"

"We will be out gunned. My brother will have an army out here to take us out." Said Dennis.

"Spread out. If we make it look like there are more of us, they may hang back."

We all spread out and watched the ridge line. It was only a small ridge but Michael's men had the high ground, which was always an advantage.

"We know they are heavily armed now so keep your eyes and ears open. We can expect them to try and keep the high ground but that means they may rain down explosives on us. Try and find some cover."

There wasn't much in the way of cover down here but we had to try and keep out of sight.

Suddenly there were cracks and pops as assault rifle rounds started peppering the area, followed by an explosion.

"Is everyone ok? Keep down."

Everyone replied through their mic's that they were ok.

"Stan. We are taking fire. The heli is down. What's your ETA?"

"We are about an hour out still. Can you hold them off?"

"We have no choice but to try. We'll look at finding another way round. They are heavily armed. Watch yourselves on the way in."

"Will do. Just keep your heads down and don't get shot."

"That's the plan."

Another explosion. "We need to look for another route. We are sitting ducks here."

"We can assume they have night vision on so they will see where we go." Said Mark.

Mark and Will were the two extra guys with us. They are good lads, and they know their stuff. I guess they wouldn't be working for Stan if they didn't.

"I agree. If we all move it will only draw more fire. We need to split up. Mark, John, you are with me. Danny, take Dennis and Will. You go right. We'll go left. Let's try and get round the sides of that ridge. Hopefully by then Stan and the others will be here." We moved off low and slow to our left and were met with more rounds.

Danny and his team fired towards the ridge to keep their heads down. Once we got to a slightly better position. We returned the favour. We kept getting peppered with rounds and the odd explosion but we were lucky enough to all be unharmed so far. We worked our way up and around the ridge. It seemed to take forever but we all got into better positions.

"We are blocked now. Our only way from here is over the ridge." Said Danny.

"Pretty much the same here. We can go a little further but the route is also blocked. They've stopped firing at us so we must be out of sight where we are."

"Same here. We can't get over that ridge without getting hit."

"Mike. We are in position on the west side. Tell us what you need."

"We are on the east side split into two teams now. Both teams are under a small ridge. The only way is over it. That's where we've been taking fire from."

"Are you still taking fire?"

"No. We must be out of sight at the moment. Same for Danny and his team on the other side."

"Ok. Stay put. We will come to you. Just keep your heads down until I tell you otherwise."

"Will do."

21

Bobby and one of his guards were looking through the plans when two men rushed into the room.

"Bobby, things are kicking off outside. Gunfire and explosions. We can't get to the back exit to check it because the main cave area is hectic right now."

"Seems like it's started. We leave through the front. We get out of the way and wait for things to calm down. Then we come and see if Michael is still standing. One of you go and get the guys. We leave here together asap."

"Yes boss" said one of the men as he rushed off.

Bobby knew that the only way to get out of this, was to keep low until it went quiet, then see who was left. Any luck, both Michael and Dennis would be dead. If not he planned to finish them himself.

It wasn't long before the guys turned up. They knew, that once they started out that cabin door, the shit would hit the fan.

"Whatever happens. I want you all to know that I appreciate your loyalty. If we make it through this, You will be rewarded. Let's go." Bobby led the way out.

They ran out of the area where his room was, and headed up to the cabin.

It didn't take them long to get there.

"Once we exit that door. We kill anyone who isn't with us. I don't care who they are."

The door faced south. Bobby wouldn't know that to his east and west were Mike's teams. He barged through the door and took out the first guard he saw. Two more guards were running past the cabin towards the east side and two of his men let them have it.

"We go west" Bobby shouted. Pointing in that direction.

They all followed him west for a matter of seconds then started taking fire.

"Keep low and fight through."

Bobby let his men take the lead and watched as a couple of them were cut down by gunfire almost immediately.

"Fuck this." He said to himself.

He left the guys to it and sloped off in a different direction.

Michael was shouting orders at his men as he tried to make sure the main cave area wasn't entered by the attackers.

"No one gets in here, no matter what."

His guys were running around taking up defensive positions ready to defend the area if needed.

"Get the vehicles ready to leave. As soon as we are ready, we will drive through that exit and take them down."

Michael had installed a hydraulic door at the back of the cave. Once the button was pressed, the fake rocks on the outside would slide apart and the door would open.

"Remember. We don't blow the explosives unless we are overrun."

Bobby tried to go south and keep away from the gun fire, his men were loyal but he was in self preservation mode now. They would fight their way out. It seemed like the gun fire was coming from all directions.

Bobby ran round to the east side of the cabin towards the ridge. There were explosions, and bullets ricocheting all over the place. Briefly Michael's guys stopped firing.

"Why has it gone quiet?" Bobby asked one of the men.

"Looks like the attackers have hidden behind the ridge. We are waiting for them to show themselves."

Bobby kept moving. He only got a few more yards when someone shouted, "GRENADE" he dived for the nearest cover, which happened to be the ridge. Landing on the other side he got to his feet and turned to see three guns pointing at him.

"It's ok. He's good" said Dennis.

Danny and Will slowly lowered their weapons.

"Am I glad to see you. What a shit storm this has turned out to be." Said Bobby.

"I thought you were locked up?"

"I was. Turns out I still have some loyal followers. They are trying to fight off, what I can only assume are more of your guys."

"Where's my brother?"

"Hiding out down in the main part of the mine."

"How many guys are we up against?" asked Danny.

"Not sure. Probably fifteen to twenty over this ridge. As for down in the mine, could be forty to fifty. I've been kept away from most of it."

Bobby thought about not telling them about all of the explosives but decided to go along with the friendly act for now. He could deal with Dennis later. He would use these guys to get rid of Michael first.

"Michael has explosives planted all over the place down there. He has a lot of weaponry too. It's not going to be a walk in the park."

"It never is" said Will.

22

John, Mark and myself, were still keeping our heads down. We thought about running into the forest area behind us and circling round that way but it was to far over open ground.

I hated just sitting here waiting. I wanted to get going and get inside. Stan came on the radio.

"You boys still ok? We are experiencing a little resistance right now. Will be with you soon."

Danny answered before I got the chance too.

"Stan. We have Bobby here with us. Those guys you are fighting could actually help us get inside."

"Well I'm open to suggestions but right now they are shooting at us."

"Ok, give me a minute."

"We need to get a message to those guys of yours. They need to stand down and work with us." Danny said to Bobby.

"We don't have radios. How do we get that message to them?" said Bobby.

"You need to go back and tell them"

"What? I'll be bloody cut down before I reach them."

"You must have passed the men on that ridge. They know who you are. Get their attention and go back passed them."

"Oh for fuck sake. This is not how I planned to get out of here."

"Once your guys stop shooting at ours, they can work together and take out those wankers who are keeping us pinned here."

"Ok, ok."

Bobby was not happy about going back over that ridge but he knew the man standing in front of him was right. He didn't care about the guys on that ridge. Having a small army behind him would better his odds of getting away from here.

He crept back up to where he had dived over previously and got the attention of one of the men.

The man acknowledged him and went back to Manning his weapon.

Bobby jumped over the top of the ridge and ran towards his guys. He had to hit the ground at one point through fear of getting ripped to pieces from the flying bullets.

"Hey" he shouted to his men. No one herd him.

"HEY" he shouted again. Two of the men turned and ran over to him.

"You ok Bobby?" one of them asked.

"Yes I'm fine. You need to stop shooting at those men. They are here to help."

"But they are firing at us boss."

"Just stop firing and get down. Trust me."

His men looked puzzled but they ran back over to the other men and started shouting at them. Eventually the men had stopped firing and got down and waited.

"Stan. Those men will stop shooting at you in a minute. They know you are here to help. Once you have all shook hands and made up, we need this ridge clearing." Said Danny.

"Understood." Came Stan's reply.

Stan stopped his team from firing and waited a moment to make sure there was no one left who hadn't heard the order to stop.

Eventually, Bobby stood up and walked slowly towards Stan's team.

"I'm Bobby" he said as he walked over to them.

"Stan."

They shook hands.

"There are men along the ridge on the other side of the cabin. They need to be taken out."

"Lead the way."

Bobby turned and walked towards the cabin. His men followed. Stan nodded at his team to follow behind. Once they were at a point where they could attack, Bobby stopped.

"Once we go round this corner we will be seen. We need to hit them fast. They are well armed. I think it's best if me and my guys go round first because they know us.

You follow behind. Once we are all round there we start shooting." Said Bobby.

"I can go with that." Said Stan.

Bobby lead his men round the corner of the cabin. Some of the men along the ridge had a quick glance at them and turned back to their weapons.

Stan and his team came round next. No one from the ridge bothered to look. Stan and Bobby nodded at each other and fired the first shots.

23

Michael was watching things unfold on the cameras. Noticing what he believed to be Bobby, running around outside infuriated him. He was supposed to be under lock and key and guarded. What was he paying these people for?

"Hey you." He shouted to one of his men. "Get out there and bring Bobby back here. Take a couple of men with you."

"Yes boss." Came the reply.

"And don't come back without him."

The man rushed off.

He thought about taking the fight outside but quickly changed his mind. He'd rigged this place for a worse case scenario and he was armed to the teeth. He would just wait for them to come to him. They would be walking into their own grave. Once he had dealt with them all, he planned to seal off this place for good. They would be dead and buried and forgotten about.

Stan radioed the guy's. "It's all clear up hear."

Myself, Mark and John slowly crept out from our position and climbed up over the ridge. Danny and his team did the same.

"Glad to see you are all in one piece." Said Stan, as the guys all walked towards them.

"Right gent's. We need to get in there, does anyone know of another way in?" I said to no one in particular.

"There is a back way but it's locked down. Apart from blowing our way in, that entrance is staying shut." Said one of Bobby's guys.

"The only way in really, is through the cabin and down onto the tunnels."

"How many tunnels are under there?"

"Two. Well, there are three but one of them is a bit of a death trap. The walls and ceiling are caving in, in places. There's a chance we may not even be able to get through it anyway. It could already be blocked off by the collapsed stone."

"Right. Well it looks like we are using the other two then. We should split up and get down there." Said Stan.

Bobby told his guys to split up and lead us through the tunnels. Bobby and Stan's team set off towards the cabin entrance, lead by Bobby's men. The rest of us followed our tour guides in behind.

The cabin wasn't much to look at. Barely any furniture or anything to suggest people used to stay here. We all walked through to the rear of the cabin and down some stairs to a basement. Once we were all in the basement Bobby's men split up and led our teams through two different tunnel entrances. They were just doorways that led through onto tunnels. There was barely enough room for two people to move through side by side, so we stuck to single file. We had only been walking through our tunnel around thirty seconds when we heard running foot steps coming towards us. We all stopped and Bobby's guys knelt down in front of us, ready to take on whoever was approaching. A few seconds went by and three men appeared from around the slight bend up ahead. They saw us and just came to an abrupt halt. They obviously knew some of the men who were leading us through, you could see the recognition on there faces. It didn't take them long to realise we were stood behind them, all weapons pointing in there direction. I could tell that their lead guy was weighing up his options. Should he take us on or put down his weapon and maybe survive. He slowly put his weapon on the floor and signalled his mates to do the same.

Bobby's men stood up and walked towards them weapons raised. They started having a conversation but I couldn't make out what was being said. Eventually the guys picked their weapons up from the floor and seemed to be joining us.

"Can we trust them?" I asked one of Bobby's men when we caught up with them.

"These men work for the highest payer. I promised them a good bonus if they lead us in. We will be fine."

I wasn't completely happy with the situation but I'd just have to keep my eye on them.

We continued down the tunnel. The air felt a lot cooler the further we went.

"Not much further now" said one of the men.

I looked at Mark and John, they looked focused. We would certainly be walking into a fight so we needed to be ready.

24

We eventually got to a T junction that turned out to be an outer ring tunnel around the main central area. I could only assume that Stan and his team were in a similar position.

"There are cameras from this point on. Once we start through here, they will see us coming." Said one of Bobby's men.

"Ok hold up" I said.

"Stan, you hear me?"

"Loud and clear. What's your status?"

"We are at the outer ring T junction, ready to move. Camera's will see us from this point on."

"Ok. We go on your word."

I got a nod from everyone, telling me they were ready to move.

"We're moving."

"Copy that."

We moved off and headed right. All we could do now was be alert and ready to take out anyone who tried to stop us. Coming up to a junction in the ring, we could clearly see this was one of the rear exits that had been blocked off. Big boulders and big chunks of concrete sealed it off.

We were about to enter the main central cave for the old mine. No matter how many fire fights you've been in, the nerves still spike when it's about to get noisy.

As one of our guides put his head round the corner he was taken out by gun fire. His brains covering the wall behind him and some of his mates.

"Stan, they are waiting for us. Had our first casualty. Watch yourselves."

"Copy that. We are going to have to use grenades to get in there."

"The whole place is rigged with explosives so I'm told."

"Yes. Bobby just confirmed that. Do you have smoke?"

"Yeah we do."

"Then we'll see you soon."

Judging by the gunfire that started a few seconds later, I guessed that Stan's team had thrown smoke grenades and went for it.

Now it was our turn.

"We go in fast. Keep your heads down. Don't get shot. We all meet on the other side of the cave."

Nods from them all was the only reply I got.

A handful of smoke grenades were tossed round the corner and we gave it a few seconds then went for it. Gunfire started straight away. It wasn't a great feeling, running through a hail of bullets, but we had to get in there. I kept taking pot shots in the direction of the gunfire and hoped that Stan and his team weren't in that area. We could here grunts and shouts as people were getting hit. Thuds and scuffles as they were falling to the floor. My guys would be right behind me, I knew that.

As the smoke started to clear we could see the damage that had been done. We lost a few of Bobby's guys and Will was down too. It was worse losing someone you know, even if they knew what they were getting into.

As we made our way through, the smoke started to clear. It seemed like it was being sucked out of the place, like a big vacuum was sucking it all out. I soon realised that a big hydraulic door was opening on the far side of the cave.

"We need to get to that door before they try to leave." I shouted over the noise.

"Well, unless you can make us all bulletproof that ain't gonna happen." Said one of the guys.

We could see more now. Vehicles were starting to manoeuvre towards the big open doorway.

They were going to get away. We couldn't let that happen again.

The vehicles were about to leave.

"Right. Change of plan. Let's get back outside. We will have to take them, out there."

I radioed Stan and told him what we were doing. We all ran towards the big hydraulic door as the last vehicle drove out.

The door started to close again.

"Shit. We aren't all gonna make it. We need to go back out the way we came in." I shouted.

Half of us turned to go back and a couple of our guys carried on hoping to make it out.

I saw one make it and his mate got his foot trapped as he tried to squeeze through the last few inches before the door slammed shut.

"EXPLOSIVES." Someone reminded us over the radio.

We all tried to make our legs run faster than they were already running.

We made it to the outer ring corridor and ran like fuck to get to the passageway to take us back outside.

As we all ran into the passageway we felt then heard the explosion. It seemed to be multiple explosions coming from behind us.

We kept pumping our arms and legs, trying to make it out before it all came crashing down.

The passageway was starting to crumble. The floor was shaking. I was starting to think that we wouldn't make it, then we could see the exit to the cabin.

25

Michael was in the first vehicle to drive out through the door. He didn't waste any time waiting to blow the explosives. Once his vehicle was a safe distance away he hit the trigger that set of an almighty explosion.

He hadn't waited to make sure all of his men got out, he just wanted to blow the place whilst Dennis's mates were still in there.

"STOP." He shouted to his driver.

"Boss, we need to get away from here." Came the reply.

"I said stop. We aren't leaving until I know they are all dead."

The driver stopped the vehicle and Michael jumped out and looked back in the direction they'd come.

He was thrilled to see smoke and flames coming from one of the other exits.

He could now see the other vehicles stopping behind his, so it looked like they had all got out in time. The door must have closed again because he couldn't see any smoke coming from that area.

"What the fuck happened to Bobby." He said to no one in particular.

No one answered.

"We wait here to see if anyone comes out. I highly doubt anyone survived that but we don't leave here until we are sure nobody made it out."

Michael ordered a group of his men to go in via the cabin and look for survivors.

My legs didn't want to move any faster than they were already, but I gave it everything I had to make it into the tunnel leading up to the cabin.

All the guys were still behind me, running for their lives.

We sprinted up the tunnel and stopped before going up to the cabin. We stood there for a few seconds, catching our breath.

"We need to go out slowly. They could be waiting for us."

Everybody nodded in agreement as they tried to get their breath back.

We started to move up, cautiously making our way to the cabin.

Approaching the door I put an ear to it and listened for a few seconds. It was hard to tell if there was anyone in there, because there was still a lot of noise coming from the cave in the mine. There were no more explosions, just lots of noise from collapsing tunnels and brickworks.

I grabbed the handle on the door and slowly turned it. There was no noise until I started to open the door. As it creaked slightly I stopped to wait for any sign of anybody the other side. I didn't have to wait. The bullets pinged off the metal and everyone dived away from the door.

I managed to slam it shut again as the bullets kept coming.

"They don't seriously think they can shoot through that do they?" said one of the guys.

"It's just a show of fire power." I said.

"Mike. You ok?" Asked Dennis.

"Well I've been in better situations mate, thanks for asking." I answered with a grin.

"I meant, with that" he said, pointing to my hand.

I looked down to see what he was talking about, only to see my pinkie was missing and my hand was covered in blood.

"Fuck sake." I said out loud, as I retrieved a bandage from my chest pocket and proceeded to wrap up my hand. Luckily for me it was my left hand not my dominant hand, so I could still fire my weapon.

"That's gonna sting mate" said one of the others.

"Let's just get in there and take them down. We still need to find Michael."

We waited for the rounds to stop pinging the door.

"As soon as those rounds stop, I will open the door and one of you needs to lob a grenade in there." I said to no one in particular.

Dennis stood next to me, grenade in hand.

"Ok. On the count of three."

I counted to two with my fingers, then on three I opened the door. Dennis lobbed the grenade in, then I slammed it shut as we all took cover. The grenade went off and a second later we were through the door.

There was no one standing in the cabin but we started taking fire from outside.

Everybody hit the floor. There wasn't much in the way of furniture to take cover behind.

Myself, John and Dennis, started firing back through the door and the window.

We exchanged fire for what seemed an age. Eventually the firing stopped. We could see no one outside from where we were.

As far as we could tell, it was all clear out front.

26

Michael wasn't expecting to here the battle that was going on at the front of the cabin.

Everyone was supposed to be killed by the blasts in the mine.

"There must be more survivors than we thought. I want everyone spread out at the rear and the sides of that cabin. None of them leave this area. I want Bobby and Dennis. Find them and bring them to me."

His men started spreading out around the area.

Michael pulled out his phone and called Dennis.

The call went unanswered.

"Where are you Dennis?" he said quietly to himself.

Myself, Dennis and John slowly made our way outside. It all seemed clear, for now at least. The others followed us out.

Once we were outside I noticed it was starting to get light. Dawn was upon us.

"We need to get this done. Let's spread out and find Michael and his men."

We all spread out and started making our way down the hill side.

It wasn't long before we bumped into Stan's team.

I noticed Stan wasn't with them.

"Where's Stan?" I asked.

"He went back in to help one of the lads and they haven't come out."

"Shit. We need to get down there and see where they are."

"No chance. That tunnel caved in behind us. We were lucky to get out."

"Fuck. They may be trapped in there."

"Trust me Mike. If they didn't get out, they are dead. There's nothing left of that route out."

"Fuck sake. Ok, let's find these bastards. We want Michael alive, for now at least."

We set off again. The hillside was made up of low trees, bushes, and dried earth that was slippery at times.

Some of us fell on our arses a couple of times.

John was now in front of me. He put up his hand to stop us.

"Get down." He whispered.

We all got down low as John came back to where I was.

"I'm pretty sure there is someone up ahead. I saw movement between the trees."

"Split up and go round then?"

"I reckon we should all go round together. Skirt to the right and try and get behind them."

"Ok. On you."

We followed John to the right keeping low. There was definitely movement through the trees.

We kept low and moved slowly around, and is wasn't long before we heard voices.

John put up his hand to stop us again.

"Definitely someone over there." John whispered, as he pointed to our left.

"Ok. You and me will take a look. Unless the shit hits the fan, the rest of you can wait here."

They all nodded.

John and I set off low and slow. We crept into the area, trying not to make any noise.

We had plenty of cover but if this person, or persons were switched on, they'd know we were coming.

After a couple more minutes we saw two men hunkered down behind a tree. They were watching the direction we were originally travelling.

We skirted a little further around so that we were directly behind them.

I signalled for John to take the one on the right as I pulled out my knife. John did the same and we snuck up behind them.

Just as we got close enough to attack I stepped on a twig and the snap made the two men turn their heads swiftly in our direction.

They were too late. By the time their heads had stopped turning I had my knife in the throat of my guy. John had taken down his guy quickly too. We waited for a few seconds then retraced our steps back to our group of men.

We split the group up into three teams then carried on around the hillside looking for Michael.

After a few minutes the shit hit the fan.

27

Unbeknown to us, there was a third man who'd stayed hidden when we took out the other two. Why he did not attack us as we left the area, we didn't know.

He stayed down until we were away from him, then he called it in.

We started taking shots from all angles. It looked like they had us surrounded. Grenades were being thrown in our direction.

I wasn't sure at that point, if we were going to make it out of there.

All our teams knew what to do, so we concentrated on our team. We agreed to fight our way out, then come back in from a different direction to find Michael.

Easier said than done.

They had us pinned. It seemed like there was no direction away from the gun fire.

We ended up picking a direction and throwing smoke grenades. Once that area was covered with smoke, we threw a couple of normal grenades then went for it.

We were shooting as we were running.

It took us a few minutes to make it to relative safety, but we got to a position where we could move out of the area.

Our fight wasn't over. As we moved, we were engaging in gunfire.

Some of the other lads had found a way out and caught up with us.

"I think we should hold off here for a bit. Give the other lads covering fire. Then we can all go ahead together." Said Danny.

"I agree mate."

We were hunkered down behind a small group of trees. There was enough space in between them that we could fire through, but enough cover to get behind when needed.

Over the next twenty minutes or so we were being joined by more of our guys.

Eventually the noise was dying down a little.

"We must have evened things out a little. We aren't taking as much fire now." Said John.

It wasn't long before all but two of our guys were back with us.

I was surprised we only lost two men, considering the amount of gunfire we were up against.

After a few more minutes we started back up the hill again.

I just wanted to find Michael and get this done.

We eventually made it back up to the flatter area at the top of the hill.

Keeping away from the cabin, we circled round behind, and down the back to where the vehicles had exited the mine.

We couldn't see where they exited from.

"Must be a hidden entrance/exit point somewhere." Said Danny.

"Must be. We should continue round and back, up towards the cabin. See if that's the way they went."

We continued round the back of the mine and started up the hill again on the other side.

Once again we started taking fire.

"Are these fuckers watching us?" said one of the guys.

"They seem to know where we are all the time"

"We should assume they are." I said.

Luckily for us there were more trees on this side of the hill, so we had better cover.

As we were fighting our way up we saw the back of a vehicle, so we guessed that must be one from the mine.

It turned out to be a line of vehicles. We were fifty, maybe sixty metres from the first vehicle we could see when the gun fire got heavier.

"They must have people guarding the vehicles"

"Looks like it. They have higher ground and vehicle cover so be careful." I shouted to our guys.

"We need to get a bit closer then we can light them up"

We pushed on slowly until we were about thirty ish metres away from the rear vehicle, then we let them have it with some grenades.

The grenades went off and set off an almighty explosion. We expected the vehicle to get blown up, but this was a much bigger bang.

We later realised that the next vehicle in front of it had been towing a small fuel bowser. That explained it. Three vehicles were actually taken out from that explosion.

This gave us the small window we needed between gunfire to push on up. Once the gun fire started again it was nowhere near as bad as it had been.

It seemed like we were winning.

28

Michael was in the lead vehicle shouting out orders and waiting for Dennis and Bobby to be found.

Once he had those two, he would clear the area then leave.

An almighty explosion made him duck down instinctively.

Once the dust had settled he jumped out of his vehicle to see what had happened.

He looked back down the line of vehicles to see that the end of the line of vehicles was just a mass of twisted metal, smoke, and flames.

"What the fuck just happened?" he shouted to his nearest man.

"We are taking fire from the rear. They must have hit the bowser."

"Fuck sake. There are more of us than them. Take them out and find me my brother."

"We are trying boss. Those people are well trained."

"Aaaaargh. I don't give a shit how well trained they are." Michael lost it and put a bullet between the guys eyes.

"You want a job doing. Better to fucking do it yourself." He said out loud.

He worked his way slowly towards the rear of the vehicle. Using the vehicle behind as cover he started taking shots towards the on coming attackers.

He got two vehicles down the line when he thought he saw Dennis.

We were working our way closer. As we were pretty much level with the twisted mess of the rear vehicles, Dennis got my attention.

"I'm pretty sure Michael is just up ahead between those vehicles. If you cover me, I'll go up and try to get his attention."

"Ok, but take someone with you."

I watched Dennis and one of our guys sneak up around the vehicles.

We carried on fighting through the mess of twisted metal. The gun fire seemed to have slowed now, just pot shots here and there.

I didn't know if we'd taken them all down, or they were just regrouping. We sat where we were for a few minutes to let things die down.

It all went quiet as we waited. Then we heard a single shot.

"That shot sounded like it came from the vehicles." Said John.

"Lets work our way up slowly. Keep your heads down."

We all moved up slowly. Half of us up one side of the vehicles, half up the other side.

By the time we'd reached the lead vehicle there was nobody in sight.

"Where's everyone gone?" said Danny.

"Fuck knows. Now the sun is up, we need to keep our heads down. You lot take the far side of the cabin, we'll go this way. Meet round the front."

The cabin was situated in the middle of the flat top of the hill. It had a clearing of around thirty metres around its perimeter, so no matter which direction you came from, you had to get across that open space to reach the cabin. We watched the other lads disappear around the other side then one at a time whilst being covered by the rest of us, we ran across the open space.

Once we were all across and standing at the side of the cabin, we started towards the front.

I was the first to the corner. I raised my hand to stop everyone and slowly peered round the corner. I shot my head back after seeing two guards outside the front door.

"Two guarding the door." I motioned to the others.

I slowly took another look, only to see Bobby walking up to the guards.

"What the fuck is he doing" I whispered to myself.

I turned to John and Danny and told them what was going on.

"We better be ready to go for it." Said John.

I took another look. Bobby was no longer there. Only one guard remained outside.

"I think he's gone inside with one of the guards."

"Maybe we should take out the remaining guard and get in there." Said Danny.

"I agree, but we don't know what we're up against.

Just then we heard a single shot from inside the cabin.

"Do we still have the crossbow?"

"Yes. I have it."

I was handed the crossbow. If I could take out this guard silently, we may still be able to keep this quiet.

I took a look round the corner, and the guard was looking nervous. He obviously knew we where out here somewhere.

I had to be quick. His eyes were alert. I had to put myself in a vulnerable position to take this shot.

I made sure the crossbow was ready to fire, then turned to face the cabin wall. I side stepped out from the corner, aimed the crossbow and took the shot. The guard was down.

29

After managing to get Dennis to the cabin without getting shot, Michael pushed him down into a chair and ordered two of his men to stand guard outside the door.
"Dennis, Dennis, Dennis. What were you thinking? Did you honestly believe you could get away with this? After all I've done for you. I practically brought you up myself because our parents were fucking useless. I looked out for you, kept you safe, and this is how you repay me."
"So, what? You going to shoot me now?"
"Well, you're no use to me now. You can't be trusted."
"We are brothers Michael, but I wasn't prepared to stand by and watch you hurt more innocent people. You killed that girl for no reason...."
Michael cut him off mid sentence.
"There is always a reason for doing what we do, brother. We were getting paid well to bring that woman to the boss...."
It was now Dennis's turn to but in.

"YOU were getting paid well. The rest of us lived on whatever you decided to give us. We were your minions, now I've had enough."

"You are in no position to give me shit Dennis. You've betrayed me, now you will pay."

Just then one of the guards came in from outside.

"STAY OUTSIDE." Shouted Michael.

"I'm sorry boss, but Bobby is outside and wants to talk to you."

"Is he really?" said Michael with a grin. "Let him in."

Bobby came through the door and just stared at the scene. He wasn't expecting to see Michael pointing a gun at his own brother.

"Nice of you to join us. I must say, you've got some balls just walking in here like this. Get over there."

Michael pointed to a chair, not far from where Dennis was sitting.

Bobby sat down and looked at Dennis.

"You ok?"

Dennis nodded.

"You are not here for a chit chat." Said Michael.

"Michael. Think about what you are doing. Lots of people have died, including my boys. This shit has to stop!"

"This, SHIT! Stops, when I decide it does."

"You aren't seriously going to shoot your own brother?"

"Bobby, you have been part of this group for years. I have put up with you because of the boss. He is no longer here, so that makes me the boss. I have no further use for you. I think it's time you joined your boys."

As Michael swung the weapon round to aim at Bobby, Dennis knew what his brother was about to do. Michael was standing to far away to reach him before he let of the shot, so he launched himself in Bobby's direction, hoping to knock him out of the way.

He managed to save Bobby, only to take the bullet himself. Straight through his thigh.

Dennis screamed as he hit the floor.

"For fuck sake Dennis. What is wrong with you? Why are you trying to protect him. He blames you as well for his boys deaths."

As Dennis sat on the floor grimacing, Bobby took off his jacket and pressed it against Dennis's thigh to try and staunch the bleeding.

"Bobby sit down." Said Michael with annoyance.

Bobby didn't move. "We have to stop the bleeding."

The shot rang out as the bullet went straight into the side of Bobby's head.

"What the fuck are you doing?" Shouted Dennis.

"He has been loyal to you for years, despite your arrogance."

"Shut up. I'm getting really bored now. You have taken up enough of my time. Give me one good reason why I shouldn't finish you off now."

"Because my friends are out there" Dennis nodded in the direction of the door. "They will be here any second now."

"Your friends" Michael laughed. "Your friends are probably all dead now. If there are any of them left, they won't be able to stop this."

30

The bullet hit Michael in the shoulder, knocking him to the floor.

By the time he'd landed on the floor we'd crashed through the door, taken out the guard, and all of our weapons were pointing at him.

"You ok Dennis?"

"This is becoming a bit of a habit." Was his reply.

His comment made me smile.

I could see that Bobby was dead. Why he'd decided to come in here like that I'll never know.

John had already kicked Michael's weapon out of the way.

Michael sat himself up against a wall as he grimaced.

"You need to say anything to your brother?" I asked Dennis.

"I have nothing more to say to him."

"You are such a pussy Dennis. No wonder our parents treated you the way they did." Michael said with a snigger.

Dennis gestured for me to give him a weapon.

I handed him the pistol from my leg holster.

"You are a piece of shit Michael. You don't deserve to live." Said Dennis through gritted teeth.

"Go on, DO IT." Jeered Michael. "You don't have the balls"

The pistol was shaking in Dennis's hand.

"I can't shoot my own brother, no matter how much of an arsehole he is."

Dennis lowered the pistol.

"You know we can't let him walk out of here" I said.

"I know." Dennis handed over the pistol to John.

"Get me out of here" he said.

Myself and Danny grabbed Dennis and helped him outside.

We heard John say something just before we heard the single shot.

It was over.

John had obviously got something off his chest that he needed to say to Michael.

John came outside, and for a moment or two he said nothing.

Dennis was the one to break the ice.

"Thank you. I thought I'd easily be able to put a bullet in him. Again, I'm sorry for what happened to Sally."

"You were trying to help her. For that I am grateful." Said John.

They shook hands and smiled at each other.

It was good to see the animosity gone between them, because despite Dennis's involvement at the start, he'd tried to do the right thing by Sally and got burned and shot twice for his troubles.

We regrouped with the rest of the guys. We checked over the vehicles for the best three to get us home, and torched the rest. We then set fire to the cabin. And drove away.

TWO MONTHS LATER

We'd had a memorial for Stan and the men we lost. Carol was distraught after we'd told her about his death. After finally being happy with life after Rufus. It was hard for her to deal with the fact Stan was gone. Harder was the fact we had no body to bury.
This place certainly wasn't going to be the same without him. Everyone here had loved Stan, a larger-than-life character, who was always ready to help. He'll be greatly missed by all who knew him.
Dennis was healing nicely from his shot up leg.
Billy was glad to have the rest of us back home.
John was now living with the girls in a house not too far from Sally's old apartment.

I still saw him and the girls regularly, but John wanted to have them in a normal home environment.

This place was quiet. We'd had no calls for help, which in some ways I was glad about. It was nice having some down time.

After letting my hand heal from the surgery for the missing finger, I'd done the tourist bit in Vegas and San Francisco.

I was loving life.

We were running the place just like Stan had.

Stan had started something good here, helping people who needed protection, or weren't getting the help they needed.

It felt good to be helping people, I was just hoping that we could start doing that in a less violent fashion.

I had been toying with the idea of leaving and doing some travelling.

There were so many beautiful places to see, but for now, at least, I'd decided to stay put and carry on doing what we do.

John had decided to be a stay at home dad for now.

He didn't need to work. He was fine financially. He just wanted some time to enjoy the twins and relax a little.

Be there for his girls whenever they needed him.

I think, that after missing so much quality time with them, he realised how much he needed to be in there lives.

Where life was going to take me from here? I didn't know. But one thing was for sure.

Whatever, or wherever it was, I planned to enjoy it..

THE END

Printed in Great Britain
by Amazon